THE DELICIOUS
BUG

WRITTEN AND ILLUSTRATED BY

JANET PERLMAN

KIDS CAN PRESS

It was a quiet and peaceful day in the forest.

shloooop!

The beaky bird was feeding berries to her babies.
The lemurs were munching on leaves.
The tomato frog was catching bugs.

splosh!

Or at least
he was trying.

They were hanging out by the pond when an especially plump and delicious-looking bumblebug flew by. Willy and Wally smacked their lips. "Mmm, lunch!" said Willy. "Yummmm!" said Wally.

flip flup flip flup

And then a rare thing happened ...

They both caught the bug at the same time!

Willy gave a little tug, and so did Wally. Before long, they were pulling each other back and forth around the forest ... over an anthill ... under a tortoise ... past a family of shrews ... and right up a tree!

Willy and Wally were getting very angry.
They tried to stare each other down.
They snarled ferociously. They puffed
themselves up and made scary faces.

By now, all the animals in the forest were watching. This had become embarrassing.

The two chameleons were furious! First there was a slap, then a pulled tail, and soon it was a full-scale battle.

They became a whirlwind of fists and feet, punching and kicking, pinching and scratching. Then they started throwing things.

The chameleons were so hopping mad that they completely forgot about the bug.

SUDDENLY, IT ESCAPED!

Willy and Wally froze.

Their bulging eyes searched frantically in all directions.

There! Just below them!

flip flup flip flup

As they scrambled to get the bug, Willy and Wally lost their balance and down they tumbled ...

DOWN

DOWN

DOWN

... straight toward the jaws
of two hungry crocodiles!

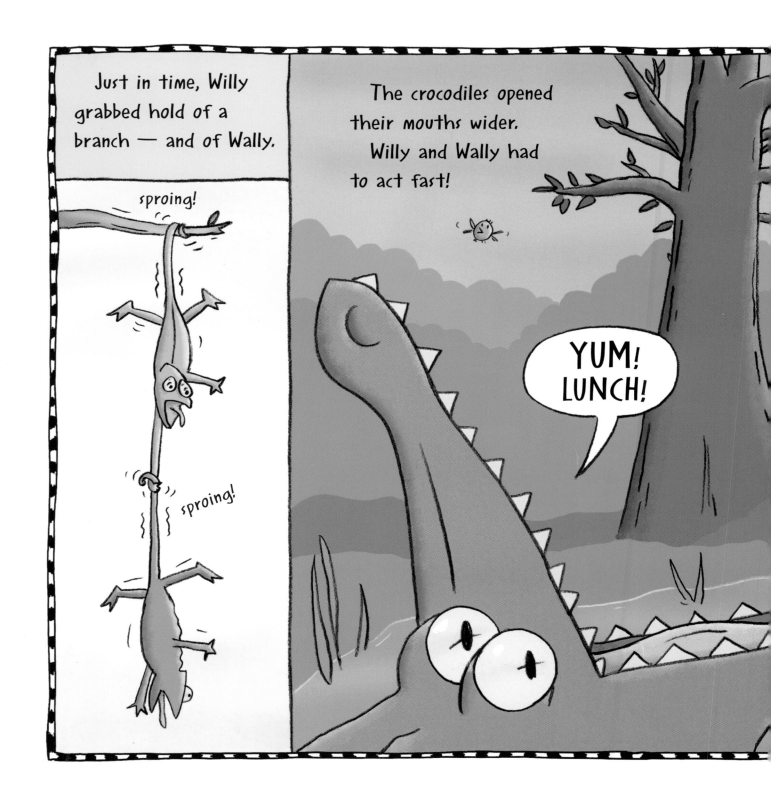

Wally had an idea. He started to swing back and forth, higher and higher ...

... until they were swinging as high as they could.

They landed safely
in a clump of leaves.

kerflumP!!

kerflomP!!

PHEW!

The chameleons felt very foolish.
How stubborn they had been!
Willy turned to Wally.
"You can have the next bug, Wally."
"That's okay, Willy. You can have it."
They said they were sorry and
shook tails, friends again.

He was just about to eat the bug when he had a great idea.

The frog laid a table with his finest dishes and silver. In the center, on a bed of water lettuce, he placed the bumblebug.

He then invited Willy and Wally for dinner.

When they were seated, the frog divided the
bug and put a share on each plate.
"This bug's on me!" he declared.

shloooop!

kersploosh!

And before long, the forest was once again a green and peaceful place.

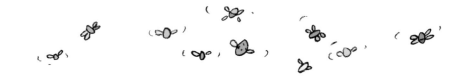

To Mark and George, who do get along fine!

A big bug salute to editor Debbie Rogosin and designer Karen Powers
for their great ideas and for helping me to get the bugs out,
and to Susan Gordon for helping to keep things buzzing.

Text and illustrations © 2009 Janet Perlman

THE DELICIOUS BUG is based on the Janet Perlman animated film
DINNER FOR TWO © 1996 by the National Film Board of Canada
and part of the ShowPeace series (http://www.nfb.ca/showpeace).

Kids Can Press acknowledges the financial support of the Government
of Ontario, through the Ontario Media Development Corporation's
Ontario Book Initiative; the Ontario Arts Council; the Canada Council
for the Arts; and the Government of Canada, through the BPIDP,
for our publishing activity.

Published in Canada by
Kids Can Press Ltd.
29 Birch Avenue
Toronto, ON M4V 1E2

Published in the U.S. by
Kids Can Press Ltd.
2250 Military Road
Tonawanda, NY 14150

www.kidscanpress.com

The artwork in this book was rendered in Photoshop.
The text is set in ICG Smile Medium.

Edited by Debbie Rogosin
Designed by Karen Powers

Printed and bound in Singapore

This book is smyth sewn casebound.

CM 09 0 9 8 7 6 5 4 3 2 1

Library and Archives Canada Cataloguing in Publication

Perlman, Janet, 1954–
    The delicious bug /written and illustrated by
Janet Perlman.

ISBN 978-1-55337-996-6

1. Chameleons — Juvenile fiction. I. Title.

PS8581.E7Z6D45 2009   jC813'.54   C2008-907216-2

Kids Can Press is a Corus™ Entertainment company